SWEET VALLEY KIDS

JESSICA
THE TV STAR

Written by
Molly Mia Stewart

Created by
FRANCINE PASCAL

Illustrated by
Ying-Hwa Hu

A BANTAM SKYLARK BOOK®
NEW YORK · TORONTO · LONDON · SYDNEY · AUCKLAND

RL 2, 005–008

JESSICA THE TV STAR
A Bantam Skylark Book / March 1991

*Sweet Valley High® and Sweet Valley Kids are trademarks of
Francine Pascal*

Conceived by Francine Pascal

*Produced by Daniel Weiss Associates, Inc.
33 West 17th Street
New York, NY 10011*

Cover art by Susan Tang

*Skylark Books is a registered trademark of Bantam Books, a division of
Bantam Doubleday Dell Publishing Group, Inc.*

ISBN 0-553-15850-3

Published simultaneously in the United States and Canada

*Bantam Books are published by Bantam Books, a division of Bantam Double-
day Dell Publishing Group, Inc. Its trademark, consisting of the words
"Bantam Books" and the portrayal of a rooster, is Registered in U.S. Patent
and Trademark Office and in other countries. Marca Registrada. Bantam
Books, 666 Fifth Avenue, New York, New York 10103.*

To Mihkaila Grodzin

CHAPTER 1

The Mix-up

Elizabeth Wakefield woke up with a stomachache. "I think I'm sick," she whispered to her twin sister, Jessica, who was asleep in the bed next to her.

"What?" Jessica said as she sat up in her bed and looked over at Elizabeth. "Do you think you have to stay home from school?"

"I don't know," Elizabeth answered. She tried to sit up, but her stomach did a roller-coaster dive. "Ugh," she said and sank back against her pillow.

Jessica got out of bed quickly and ran to the door. "I'll get Mom."

While Jessica was getting Mrs. Wakefield, Elizabeth closed her eyes. She felt terrible.

"Don't you feel well, honey?" Mrs. Wakefield asked as she entered the twins' room. She sat down on the side of Elizabeth's bed.

"No," Elizabeth said. She looked at her mother and then at her sister. Jessica was standing by the bed.

The twins did so many things together that it was difficult for them to understand that one could feel sick and the other could feel OK. They shared their bedroom and they picked out their clothes together. Each often knew what the other was thinking.

From the outside, no one could tell the two girls apart. Both had long blond hair with bangs, and both had blue-green eyes. When they dressed exactly alike, the only way to tell them apart was by looking at their name bracelets. Sometimes they pretended they were each other to tease their friends and their brother, Steven.

Even though they looked the same on the outside, Elizabeth and Jessica were very different on the inside. Elizabeth liked to play sports such as soccer and to play adventure games outside. She also loved doing her homework, and she spent her free time reading books.

Jessica was just the opposite. She hated getting her clothes dirty. She preferred ballet and playing with dolls indoors. She didn't like school very much, and hated doing her homework.

None of the differences mattered to Jessica and Elizabeth, though. Being twins was special. The two girls were best friends.

"I think I'll keep you in bed today," Mrs. Wakefield said as she felt Elizabeth's forehead. "You feel warm."

"Can I stay home, too?" Jessica asked. "I might be getting a stomachache any minute."

Mrs. Wakefield shook her head and smiled. "No, Jess. I'm afraid you have to go to school."

Jessica grumbled all the way through breakfast. "You'll be so lonely today," she said to Elizabeth as she put on her sweater. "I should really stay home and keep you company."

"I'll be OK," Elizabeth said. Then she saw

4

something shiny fall to the floor. "Your bracelet, Jess. You'll lose it."

"Oh, no!" Jessica picked her name bracelet up off the floor. The clasp was loose. "I'll have to ask Mom to get it fixed again," she said, remembering the time she had almost lost it on the class trip to the zoo. "I don't want to lose it."

Jessica carefully placed the bracelet on the dresser. "Now no one will know whether I'm Jessica or Elizabeth today," she said with a giggle. "Bye, Liz. I hope you feel better."

Jessica ran out of the house and walked to the bus stop, feeling grumpy. It didn't seem fair for her to have to go to school alone.

"Hi, Elizabeth!"

Jessica turned around. Caroline Pearce was hurrying to catch up with her. At first,

6

Jessica was going to tell Caroline that she was Jessica and not Elizabeth. But then she decided not to.

"Hi, Caroline," she said in a friendly way, just like Elizabeth always did.

"Where's Jessica?" Caroline asked. Caroline always wanted to know where everyone was. A lot of her classmates teased her for being nosy and for trying to be the teacher's pet. She always wanted to erase the blackboard and hand out tests. Jessica didn't like Caroline very much, so it was even more fun to play a joke on her.

"Jessica is sick today," Jessica said. "Poor Jess. I feel sorry for her."

"She'll have to do extra work when she comes back," Caroline said.

As the two girls arrived at the bus stop,

7

some other girls walked over. "Hi, Elizabeth," they said when they saw Jessica standing with Caroline. Everyone knew *Jessica* was always teasing Caroline, so they were certain she was *Elizabeth*.

Jessica smiled to herself. Maybe it would be fun to pretend to be Elizabeth for one whole day, she decided.

CHAPTER 2

The Twin Switch

Jessica walked into her second-grade classroom and looked around. The first person she saw was her best friend after Elizabeth, Lila Fowler. She wanted to say hello but stopped herself. She knew that *Elizabeth* thought Lila was stuck-up and would never go talk to Lila. So instead, Jessica walked across the room to the hamster cage, where Amy Sutton, Elizabeth's best friend after Jessica, was standing.

"Hi, Amy," Jessica said.

Amy looked up. She opened her mouth to

say something, and then stopped. "Hi. Elizabeth?"

"Can't you tell us apart?" Jessica teased. "You know I'm Elizabeth."

Amy quickly glanced down at Jessica's wrist to check the name bracelet. It wasn't there because Jessica had left it on her dresser. Amy shrugged.

"Sometimes I forget how much you and Jessica look alike. I almost thought you were Jessica."

"Nope," Jessica said cheerfully.

"Take your seats, everyone," Mrs. Otis said when the bell rang. Jessica sat down in her usual seat, but then popped up again. If she was going to pretend to be Elizabeth, she would have to sit in Elizabeth's chair! She moved over one seat.

"Psst," came a voice from behind her. "Elizabeth."

Jessica turned around. Todd Wilkins was sitting behind her and one seat over.

"I need to tell you something at recess," Todd whispered. "It's a secret. Meet me at the seesaws, OK?"

Jessica smiled. "OK." She could hardly wait to know what secret Todd wanted to tell Elizabeth.

When class was over, Jessica hurried to the seesaws and waited for Todd to arrive.

"Let's go over there," Todd whispered, pointing to a tree. "I don't want anyone else to hear."

Jessica's eyes sparkled as she followed Todd.

When they were alone, Todd looked

11

around once more to be sure the coast was clear. Then he began, "A man my parents know is making an afternoon special for TV. He's going to use our house for one part of the movie!"

"Really?" Jessica gasped.

"Plus," Todd went on happily, "I get to be in it."

"Really?" Jessica said even louder. "I wish I could . . ."

"Shh!" Todd said. "Not so loud." Then he went on. "Plus they need a girl in the scene so I get to ask one girl I know to be in it. I wanted to ask you first, Elizabeth."

Jessica stared at Todd. She wanted to be in a television movie more than anything in the world, but he wasn't asking *her.*

"Um . . ." she began. "I think Jessica

would love to be on TV. She would really, really, really want to do it."

"I don't want to ask Jessica," Todd said. "You know how she is."

"What do you mean?" Jessica asked, trying not to sound angry.

"Nothing," Todd said. "It's just that I want you to be in it."

Jessica looked down at the ground. It made her feel sad to think that Todd didn't want her. Still she had to continue pretending she was Elizabeth, or Todd would be really angry at her. "Can Jessica be in it, too?" she asked.

Todd shook his head. "No. And you have to promise not to tell her—not to tell anyone. My mom and dad don't want everybody at school coming over and getting in the way."

14

"Oh." Jessica folded her arms and tried to think fast.

"You have to come over after school tomorrow," Todd went on. "That's when we're going to rehearse. Just like for our Thanksgiving play. They call it the run-through. And then we do it for real the day after that."

"OK," Jessica answered slowly. She bit her lip. Maybe if she didn't tell Elizabeth, she could go to Todd's house and keep pretending. That way she'd be in the TV movie.

"Remember, don't tell anyone, Elizabeth," Todd said.

Jessica nodded. She wasn't going to tell a single person.

CHAPTER 3

Jessica's Secret

Elizabeth woke up from her nap and looked at the clock. She realized that it was time for Jessica to come home from school. She sat up and then smiled. Her stomach felt much better. She jumped out of bed and ran to the window. She could see Jessica walking slowly toward the house.

"Hi," Elizabeth said when Jessica came upstairs to their room.

Jessica didn't look at her. "Hi," she mumbled.

"What did you do in school today?" Elizabeth asked.

"Nothing much," Jessica said with a shrug. "It was just a plain old day."

"Did anyone ask where I was?" Elizabeth went on. She had felt lonely by herself, and she missed her friends.

Jessica put her books on the desk. "Well, um, yes, I guess so. Do you feel better?"

"A lot," Elizabeth said.

"Good. How about playing dress-up?" Jessica suggested. "We can get the Halloween costumes out of the box and put them on."

"OK!" Elizabeth said. She looked at her sister. She could tell that Jessica had something on her mind. "Are you sure nothing happened at school?" she asked again.

Jessica shook her head quickly. "I said no. Come on. Let's get the costumes."

Elizabeth shrugged and followed her twin up to the attic. They dragged the large cardboard box down the stairs, making it go *bump-bump-bump* down the steps. Elizabeth and Jessica both laughed when the box tipped over and spilled the colorful costumes onto the hall floor.

"Put this on," Jessica said, picking up a cowboy hat.

"I look like Buffalo Bill!" Elizabeth said. She galloped up and down the hall on a make-believe horse. "Now I'm a cowgirl!" she yelled.

"Don't you think it's fun pretending to be a different person?" Jessica asked as she put on a super-hero cape. She did a karate kick in the air.

Elizabeth smiled. "Sure."

"You do?" Jessica looked very happy. "Wouldn't it be fun to try to make people think you were someone else?" she asked.

"You mean like what an actor does?" Elizabeth said. "Sure. I'll bet being in a movie or on TV would really be fun."

Suddenly, Jessica looked very sad. "You do?"

"Yes. Why?" Elizabeth asked, feeling puzzled.

Jessica shook her head. "I don't know."

Elizabeth shrugged. "OK." Her sister was acting strange. Elizabeth knew that soon Jessica would tell her what was bothering her.

* * *

Elizabeth felt fine the next morning, and Mrs. Wakefield let her go to school.

During attendance, Todd tapped Elizabeth on the shoulder. "Psst," he said.

Elizabeth turned around. Todd was one of the friends she had missed when she was absent. "Hi."

"Don't forget about you know what," he whispered. Todd made his eyes very wide.

Elizabeth blinked in surprise. "What?" she asked.

"Shh!" Todd moved his eyes to the left and the right, to remind her there were other people around.

"This afternoon," he said softly. "Don't forget. I'll see you after school, right?"

Next to Elizabeth, Jessica began to cough loudly and moved around in her chair.

Elizabeth looked at Jessica. Then she stared at Todd. *He was acting strange,* she thought. They had soccer-league practice after school, but Todd made it seem like a big mystery.

"Yes," Elizabeth whispered back. "I'll see you there." She turned around to face the blackboard again. Then she glanced at Jessica. Her sister was staring straight ahead, and her cheeks were pink. She looked as if she was trying not to cough.

"Are you OK?" Elizabeth asked Jessica.

Jessica nodded. "Fine," she said without looking at her.

Elizabeth shook her head and took out her notebook. People sure were acting strange today!

CHAPTER 4

Just Like Jessica

As soon as Jessica got home from school, she changed into jeans and a green T-shirt, one of Elizabeth's favorite outfits.

"I'm going to ride my bike to Todd's house!" she called to her older brother, Steven.

"No, you're not," Steven said, walking into the room. "Mom left me in charge when she took Elizabeth to soccer practice. I say you can't go."

Jessica stuck her tongue out at him. Steven could boss her around as much as he wanted, but it didn't matter to Jessica. She knew her brother was just showing off. "Todd lives only a few blocks away and I'm going."

"All right. But I'm calling his house in one hour if you're not home by then," Steven warned.

Jessica got on her bike and rode over to the Wilkinses' house. There were cars and vans parked up and down the street, and people kept going in and out the front door. Jessica walked right in.

"Elizabeth! I'm glad you're here!" Mrs. Wilkins called out, as she waved to Jessica from the living room.

Jessica's eyes were round with excitement. All of the people moving furniture and hurrying back and forth with lights were part of the television crew. It was very exciting.

"Hi," Todd said. He looked nervous.

"Hi," Jessica said to Todd. She couldn't stop staring at everything.

"That's Mr. Phillips, the director," Todd said, pointing to a short man in jeans and an old sweatshirt.

Jessica made a face. "Are you sure? He doesn't look very important."

"Positive," Todd said.

"OK, folks," Mr. Phillips said. "Let's do a run-through. Where are the kids?"

"Here!" Jessica yelled, rushing forward. "What do I do?" she asked.

Mr. Phillips came over and put his hands on Jessica's shoulders. "You and Todd will be sitting on the floor, watching TV. Then the phone will ring," he said, pointing to a white telephone.

"That's not our real phone," Todd said.

"Right," the director said. "It's called a prop. When that phone rings, I want Todd to answer it and say 'Lewis residence. Mickey speaking.' Got that?"

"What do I do?" Jessica asked before Todd could answer.

"You keep watching TV," Mr. Phillips said.

Jessica was disappointed. It didn't sound like half as much fun as what Todd was going to do.

"Let's try it," Mr. Phillips said.

A woman turned on the television set and then showed Jessica and Todd where to sit. Jessica sat down and looked at the TV.

"Just relax, Elizabeth," Mr. Phillips told her.

28

The telephone rang. Jessica jumped up at the same time that Todd did, and they both grabbed the phone.

"Not you!" Todd whispered while they each tried to grab the receiver.

"We're letting Todd answer the phone, Elizabeth," Mr. Phillips reminded her.

"Sorry, I forgot," Jessica said.

Pouting, Jessica sat down.

Todd sat down next to her again. "You're acting just like Jessica," he whispered.

"What do you mean?" Jessica asked in a shocked voice.

Todd made a face. "You know. Bossy."

Jessica's feelings were hurt, and she started to feel angry at Todd for saying something mean about her. She moved away from him and pretended he wasn't there.

29

"OK. Let's try it again," the director said.

Jessica raised her hand. "Could we try it once with me answering the phone?"

"You're going to say, 'Mickey speaking'?" Todd said with a laugh.

Jessica stuck her tongue out at him.

"Let's just try it the way we planned it, Elizabeth," Mr. Phillips said patiently. Are you ready?"

Jessica didn't know whether to be angry or excited. Even if she didn't get to answer the phone, she was still in a TV movie!

Every time she remembered Todd saying that she was bossy, she felt sad and angry all over again. Pretending to be Elizabeth was fun, but she didn't like what she was learning about Jessica!

31

CHAPTER 5

A Confusing Day

The next morning, Elizabeth and Jessica walked to the bus stop together. Todd was already there, talking to a group of boys.

"Todd never went to soccer practice yesterday," Elizabeth said to Jessica. It seemed strange to her that he hadn't been there since he had told her that he would see her after school. "I wonder why."

Jessica kicked a pebble. "I don't know."

"Hey, Todd," Elizabeth said, marching up to the group of boys. "What were you going to tell me yesterday afternoon?"

Todd's eyes widened. "Not here!" he whispered.

"Why?" Elizabeth asked in astonishment.

Todd stared at her. "Look at all the people around," he whispered angrily.

"People?" Elizabeth repeated. She was so confused that she didn't know what to say. She was beginning to feel a little angry at Todd for the way he was acting. First he wanted to talk, then he didn't want to talk. It didn't make sense. Elizabeth turned around and walked away.

"I'm angry at Todd," Elizabeth told her sister.

Jessica nodded. "Me, too."

"Why?" Elizabeth asked in surprise. "Why are *you* angry at Todd?"

"Umm . . ." Jessica looked around. "Because you are, that's why. Here comes the bus," she said, as she quickly ran to get on.

Elizabeth looked at Jessica. Todd wasn't the only person around who was acting mixed up, she decided.

CHAPTER 6

The Big Huge Secret

Jessica took her seat on the school bus and stared straight ahead. More than anything in the world, she wished she could tell someone about the TV movie. It was the biggest secret she had ever kept, especially from her twin. But if she told Elizabeth, she'd have to admit that she took away her part in the movie.

By the time the bus arrived at school, Jessica had a plan. She rushed to the classroom and found Lila. "Come here," she whispered, heading for the back of the classroom.

Lila followed her. "What is it?"

"It's a super-huge secret," Jessica said. "You have to promise you won't tell a single person in the whole world."

"OK!" Lila agreed with a smile. Lila loved secrets as much as Jessica did.

"You have to promise especially not to tell Todd or Elizabeth," Jessica added.

Lila crossed her heart. "Promise. What is it?"

"I'm going to be on TV!" Jessica said in a dramatic voice.

"What?" Lila gasped. "I don't believe you!"

"It's true. Some TV people are making a movie at Todd's house. It's for an afternoon movie. And I'm in it. So is Todd. And we're shooting for real after school today," she said proudly.

"Wow." Lila gulped and looked at Jessica with respect. "Can I come watch?"

Jessica thought for a moment. *One* person wouldn't matter, she decided. "OK, but remember. Don't tell anyone else."

"I won't," Lila promised.

Jessica went to her desk and sat down. She was glad she had told Lila. Lila's father knew a lot of famous and important people, and Lila got to do a lot of exciting things. Now it was Lila's turn to be impressed, Jessica decided.

Jessica looked around the classroom. She saw her other best friend, Ellen Riteman, walk in. Maybe she could tell just one more person.

"Ellen!" she said, running over to her. She

pulled Ellen over to a corner of the class-room.

"What's wrong?" Ellen asked in surprise.

"I have to tell you something important," Jessica said in a low, mysterious voice.

"A secret?" Ellen asked hopefully.

Jessica nodded. "First you have to promise not to tell anyone," she said. "I'm only telling you because you're my friend. You can't mention it at all, especially to Todd or Elizabeth."

"I promise," Ellen said, looking excited.

"I'm going to be on TV!" Jessica said with a big smile. "I'm the star of an afternoon movie special."

"Really?" Ellen's voice went up in a squeak.

"We're making it at Todd's house after

41

school today," Jessica went on. "The director gave me the biggest part."

Jessica felt a little bit worried because the story she was telling wasn't exactly true. But it was much more exciting than what was really happening. She didn't want to say that Todd was the only one who had lines in their scene. And she didn't want to say that the scene was very short. Jessica preferred to describe it her way.

"Can I watch?" Ellen begged. "Please? I won't get in the way, honest."

Jessica smiled. "Sure. But remember— don't tell anyone."

CHAPTER 7

Elizabeth Investigates

Elizabeth and Jessica had their usual snack when they got home from school. Elizabeth poured two glasses of milk, while Jessica took out some cookies.

"Remember how I said I was angry at Todd?" Elizabeth said.

Jessica stopped with a cookie halfway to her mouth. "Yes?" she said slowly.

"Every time I tried to talk to him today, he started acting strange," Elizabeth went on. She shook her head. "He kept saying stuff like, 'not here! not now!' I think I'm going to go over to his house and ask him what's going on."

"NO!" Jessica yelled.

Elizabeth looked at her. "Why not?"

"Because . . ." Jessica wriggled in her chair. "I . . . I heard him say he had a dentist appointment. And then, I think his grandmother is coming over." Jessica bit into her cookie and didn't say anything else. Her cheeks were pink.

"Oh." Elizabeth took a sip of milk. "I'll wait until tomorrow, then." She stood up and went to the door. "I'm going to do my homework, and then read my new book."

"Good idea," Jessica said with a big smile. "I won't bother you. I'll do something else."

"OK," Elizabeth said. She went upstairs

with her schoolbooks and started on her homework.

When she was all done, she looked out the window. It was such a nice, sunny afternoon that she thought it would be fun to play outside instead of reading. She closed her notebook and ran downstairs.

"Mom?" she called out.

Mrs. Wakefield was in the living room. "Yes, Jessica?"

"Mom!" Elizabeth laughed, sitting down next to her.

"Oh, Elizabeth." Mrs. Wakefield made a face and smiled. "I thought you went out with Steven a while ago."

Elizabeth shook her head. "I was doing homework."

"That's funny." Mrs. Wakefield said. "I

guess it was Jessica, then. Steven said he was walking her over to Todd's house to play basketball. He'll be back any minute."

"Todd's house?" Elizabeth repeated. "Basketball?"

"I could have sworn he'd said, 'Come on, Liz.' But it must have been Jessica," Mrs. Wakefield said. "We can ask him when he returns."

Elizabeth felt angry. Hadn't Jessica said that Todd wouldn't be home? Elizabeth was so upset she didn't know what to think. But she was going to find out.

"Mom, can I ride to Todd's house right now?" Elizabeth asked quickly. "I'll go straight there."

The twins weren't allowed to ride their

bikes very far alone. Since Todd's house was so close, Mrs. Wakefield agreed.

"Just be sure you and Jessica are back in time for dinner," Mrs. Wakefield said.

Elizabeth smiled, but inside she was thinking about Jessica and Todd and how they had both been acting strange lately.

Elizabeth went outside, picked up her bike, and pedaled slowly to Todd's house. She saw vans and cars blocking the street. There seemed to be a crowd of people, too. It looked like they were all right in front of the Wilkinses' house.

"Is there a big party?" Elizabeth wondered out loud.

She rode a little closer. She could see electrical wire running from the trucks right in-

side the Wilkinses' front door. The inside of the house looked filled with people. *Jessica must be there, too,* Elizabeth thought.

What is going on? she wondered.

CHAPTER 8

The Secret Is Out

When Jessica saw how many kids had showed up at Todd's house to watch the filming, she knew she was in big trouble. She tiptoed upstairs.

"Watch that cable!" someone shouted at her.

"Excuse me, you'll have to wait outside!" ordered a loud voice. Jessica peeked through the banister.

"Todd's a friend of mine," Ken Matthews was saying to a man holding a hammer. "He invited us over."

"Where's Elizabeth," Mr. Phillips asked. "What are all these kids doing here?"

Jessica squeezed her eyes shut. Either Lila or Ellen invited all these people. Jessica knew it was her fault, though. What a mess she had gotten herself into.

Elizabeth leaned her bike on its kickstand and looked around. People were running back and forth, carrying big electrical cables as well as lighting and camera equipment. She could see almost all the kids in Mrs. Otis's second-grade class.

"What's going on?" Elizabeth asked Caroline.

"Movie stars!" Caroline said in a hushed voice. "There are movie stars coming."

Elizabeth looked at the house in surprise. "Movie stars?" She walked a few steps closer, and Todd came running out of the house. He saw Elizabeth and rushed over to her.

"Elizabeth!" he yelled, sounding angry.

"What is going on?" Elizabeth asked, walking toward him. She had to step aside when a woman with a clipboard rushed by her.

Todd glared at her. "I told you not to tell anybody! My mom and dad are really mad at me, and I'm really mad at you! Mr. Phillips is angry at everybody."

Elizabeth was so startled that she didn't know what to say.

"Every girl in our class keeps asking me how come I didn't ask them!" Todd went on. "I'm sorry I ever asked you, now! I should have known this would turn into a big mess." He turned around and stomped away.

"Wait a second!" Elizabeth said. She ran after Todd. "I don't know what you're talking about!"

Todd made a face. "Oh, sure. You didn't tell anyone at school?"

"Tell them *what*?" Elizabeth held her hands up and shook her head. "I didn't tell anybody anything because I don't know what I wasn't supposed to tell!"

"But—" Todd stopped talking and stared at her. He looked upset. "But you were right here with me and Mr. Phillips yesterday when we did the run-through and everything."

Elizabeth stared at Todd and shook her head. "Todd, I don't—" Suddenly, she put one hand over her mouth and gasped. She had the answer.

54

Todd's mouth dropped open. He started shaking his head from side to side. "It wasn't you yesterday, was it? When I told you in school on Tuesday—"

"I was *absent* on Tuesday," Elizabeth said.

"Oh, no," Todd said. "Wait till I find Jessica! I thought she was you, and I wanted you to be in the movie with me, and she came over yesterday—"

"I was at soccer practice yesterday," Elizabeth said. "She didn't want me to come over to your house today, and she's already here— somewhere."

"She's going to get in trouble," Todd said.

They both charged in through the front door, shouting the same thing.

"*Jessica!*"

55

CHAPTER 9

Lights! Camera! Action!

Jessica thought it was just about time to go downstairs and see what was happening. She began to tiptoe down the steps.

"Jessica!" yelled two voices at once.

Jessica froze. Staring up at her from the bottom of the staircase were Elizabeth and Todd. They both looked angry!

"Umm . . ." she said.

"What's the big idea?" Elizabeth started to say. But before she could go on, Mr. Phillips came into the hallway from the living room. He took Elizabeth and Todd by the hand.

"Come on, kids! Let's get moving here. We're all set up and ready," he said.

"Mr. Phillips, wait," Todd said.

Mr. Phillips looked up and noticed Jessica standing at the top of the stairs. Jessica gave him an apologetic smile and waved one hand. The director blinked in surprise and looked at Elizabeth again.

"Twins?" he said. He let out a laugh. "Well, what do you know! Which one of you is Elizabeth?"

"I am," Elizabeth said. "But I think Jessica is the one you know."

Mr. Phillips shook his head. "No, you're the one I know."

Todd shook his head. "No, Jessica was Elizabeth yesterday."

"Hold on a minute, kids!" the director said. "Who was here yesterday?"

"Me," Jessica said, raising her hand.

"And you're not Elizabeth?" Mr. Phillips asked.

Jessica shook her head no.

"Well, this is getting complicated," Mr. Phillips said with a laugh. "I guess I'll use all three of you."

Elizabeth turned around and stared at him. "But . . ."

"Come on, Liz," Jessica said as she ran down the stairs and took Elizabeth's hand. "Let's do what he says!"

"But . . ." Elizabeth began.

Jessica knew her sister was very angry at her. But everyone was suddenly in a hurry, and there wasn't any time to say anything. They all followed the director into the living room.

"Look at this, everyone!" Mr. Phillips said. "We've got twins! A nice touch, I think."

The living room was full of adults bustling around with lights and cameras and microphones. All the furniture was rearranged, too. Elizabeth stood and stared. "Wow!" she said, looking excited.

"Now, Elizabeth," Mr. Phillips said. "Remember what we did yesterday?"

"No, I wasn't—" Elizabeth began.

"Right!" The director slapped one hand to his forehead. "OK! From the top. Kids, sit down in front of the television."

Elizabeth, Todd, and Jessica sat down.

"When the phone rings, Todd is going to answer it," Jessica whispered to Elizabeth.

"How do you know the phone is going to ring?" Elizabeth whispered back.

Jessica giggled. "It's a fake phone. Watch."

Mr. Phillips stood behind a big movie camera to see how they looked. "OK. We're rolling."

Jessica's heart was beating loudly in her chest. She watched the television and tried not to notice all the people around her. Suddenly the telephone rang.

"Lewis residence. Mickey speaking," Todd said when he picked it up.

"And, cut!" Mr. Phillips said. "Perfect, Todd. You did a great job. Now let's try it again. This time, I'd like Elizabeth . . ."

"Which Elizabeth?" Jessica interrupted.

Mr. Phillips grinned. "The real one, please. Let's have Elizabeth and Todd fight over who gets to answer the phone. The way you did yesterday."

"But—" Jessica said. Her big smile disappeared. It looked like Elizabeth was going to get a bigger part in the scene, and all because Jessica had tried grabbing the phone in the run-through!

"OK," Elizabeth said.

"Places, everyone. And . . . action!" Mr. Phillips pointed to them.

The three kids watched the television, and when the phone rang, Elizabeth and Todd both jumped up to answer it. Todd grabbed it away first and said his line.

"Lewis residence. Mickey speaking."

"And cut!" Mr. Phillips shouted. "Perfect! That's a wrap!"

A woman with short red hair walked over to them and handed them each a piece of paper. "Girls, you have to get your parents to sign this form, giving their permission for you to be in this movie. OK?"

Jessica folded her sheet and nodded. "OK."

"Is that all?" Elizabeth asked in surprise. "It's easy being a movie star. Right, Jess?"

Jessica shrugged. She felt grumpy about having such a small part. This whole day was not working out the way she had planned.

CHAPTER 10

Jessica Learns a Lesson

"Come on," Elizabeth said to Jessica. "We want to talk to you."

When the twins and Todd got outside, Jessica looked from Elizabeth to Todd and back again. "You aren't mad at me, are you?"

"I am!" Todd said. "You were pretending to be Elizabeth the whole time. Then you told my secret to everyone."

"I'm mad at you, too!" Elizabeth said. "You knew Todd wanted me to be in the movie and you weren't going to tell me!"

Jessica gulped. "But, well, I'm mad at you!" she said to Todd. "You said mean things about me!"

"I didn't say them to you," Todd said. He looked embarrassed.

Elizabeth frowned. "What mean things did you say about Jessica?" she asked. She didn't like anyone to criticize her sister.

"He said I was acting bossy!" Jessica said. "That's mean!"

"It is, but it's sort of true sometimes," Elizabeth said. "How come you pretended to be me when I was absent from school?" Elizabeth asked. She still felt hurt that Jessica would do that.

"It was only a joke," Jessica said honestly. "You and I like to pretend we're each other. And when I left my name bracelet at home, people thought I was you. I only meant it as a game. And then, and then . . . I couldn't stop. I didn't think it would cause so much trouble. I'm sorry, Liz," Jessica said.

"I forgive you," Elizabeth said, rubbing her sneaker on the ground. "Besides, I think you learned your lesson."

"Hey, there you are!" called out Lila. "How did it go?"

The whole group of kids from class ran over at once. They had been outside the whole time.

"Did you really get to be the star, Jessica?" Ken Matthews asked.

Jessica was smiling happily. "I wasn't exactly the star, but I had an important part in the scene," she bragged.

"Oh, brother," Todd said.

Elizabeth smiled. *Jessica would always be Jessica,* she decided. And she would always be Elizabeth. They could never, ever really be each other, because they were so different.

"When I'm a movie star, I'm going to be very rich and famous," Jessica was telling everyone. "I'm going to have a lot of very expensive things."

"Like what?" Ellen asked her.

"Tons of stuff," Jessica said, sticking her nose in the air. "Beautiful things like— like—a glass unicorn," she said suddenly. "I'll be able to get a glass unicorn any time I want to."

"Who'd want something like that?" Winston Egbert asked.

Everyone began to argue about unicorns.

Some kids liked them, some kids thought they were dumb. Then Caroline spoke up.

"I have a collection of porcelain dolls," she said proudly. "They're very delicate and very valuable."

Lila looked at her. "Oh, really?"

"Yes," Caroline said with a smile. "I have a special shelf for them at home. With lights."

"I don't believe you," Ellen said.

"That's right," Ken agreed. "Prove it."

Caroline looked angry. "I don't have to prove anything."

"Well, if you don't want to show them to us," Jessica said, "we won't believe you. I say you have to bring your porcelain dolls to school."

Caroline suddenly looked very worried.

"But my mother won't let me do that," she said.

"You're just trying to find an excuse," Lila said. "It's probably all a big lie, anyway. So there."

Does Caroline really have a collection of porcelain dolls? Find out in Sweet Valley Kids #17, CAROLINE'S MYSTERY DOLLS.

SWEET VALLEY KIDS

Jessica and Elizabeth have had lots of adventures in *Sweet Valley High* and *Sweet Valley Twins*...now read about the twins at age seven! You'll love all the fun that comes with being seven—birthday parties, playing dress-up, class projects, putting on puppet shows and plays, losing a tooth, setting up lemonade stands, caring for animals and much more! It's all part of SWEET VALLEY KIDS. Read them all!

☐ SURPRISE! SURPRISE! #1	15758-2	$2.75/$3.25
☐ RUNAWAY HAMSTER #2	15759-0	$2.75/$3.25
☐ THE TWINS' MYSTERY TEACHER # 3	15760-4	$2.75/$3.25
☐ ELIZABETH'S VALENTINE # 4	15761-2	$2.75/$3.25
☐ JESSICA'S CAT TRICK # 5	15768-X	$2.75/$3.25
☐ LILA'S SECRET # 6	15773-6	$2.75/$3.25
☐ JESSICA'S BIG MISTAKE # 7	15799-X	$2.75/$3.25
☐ JESSICA'S ZOO ADVENTURE # 8	15802-3	$2.75/$3.25
☐ ELIZABETH'S SUPER-SELLING LEMONADE #9	15807-4	$2.75/$3.25
☐ THE TWINS AND THE WILD WEST #10	15811-2	$2.75/$3.25
☐ CRYBABY LOIS #11	15818-X	$2.75/$3.25
☐ SWEET VALLEY TRICK OR TREAT #12	15825-2	$2.75/$3.25
☐ STARRING WINSTON EGBERT #13	15836-8	$2.75/$3.25
☐ JESSICA THE BABY-SITTER #14	15838-4	$2.75/$3.25
☐ FEARLESS ELIZABETH #15	15844-9	$2.75/$3.25
☐ JESSICA THE TV STAR #16	15850-3	$2.75/$3.25
☐ CAROLINE'S MYSTERY DOLLS #17	15870-8	$2.75/$3.25
☐ BOSSY STEVEN #18	15881-3	$2.75/$3.25
☐ JESSICA AND THE JUMBO FISH #19	15936-4	$2.75/$3.25
☐ THE TWINS GO TO THE HOSPITAL #20	15912-7	$2.75/$3.25
☐ THE CASE OF THE SECRET SANTA (SVK Super Snooper #1)	15860-0	$2.95/$3.50

Bantam Books, Dept. SVK, 414 East Golf Road, Des Plaines, IL 60016

Please send me the items I have checked above. I am enclosing $_____ (please add $2.50 to cover postage and handling). Send check or money order, no cash or C.O.D.s please.

Mr/Ms _____

Address _____

City/State _____ Zip _____

SVK-9/91

Please allow four to six weeks for delivery.
Prices and availability subject to change without notice.